THINGS I LIKE
ANTHONY BROWNE

WALKER BOOKS
AND SUBSIDIARIES
LONDON · BOSTON · SYDNEY

THIS WALKER BOOK BELONGS TO:

_____

_____

_____

_____

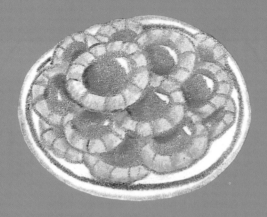

First published 1989 by Walker Books Ltd
87 Vauxhall Walk, London SE11 5HJ

This edition published 1997

4 6 8 10 9 7 5 3

© 1989 Anthony Browne

This book has been typeset in Melior Educational.

Printed in Hong Kong

British Library Cataloguing in Publication Data
A catalogue record for this book is available
from the British Library.

ISBN 0-7445-5442-X

This is me
and this is what I like:

Painting ...

and riding my bike.

Playing with toys ...

and dressing up.

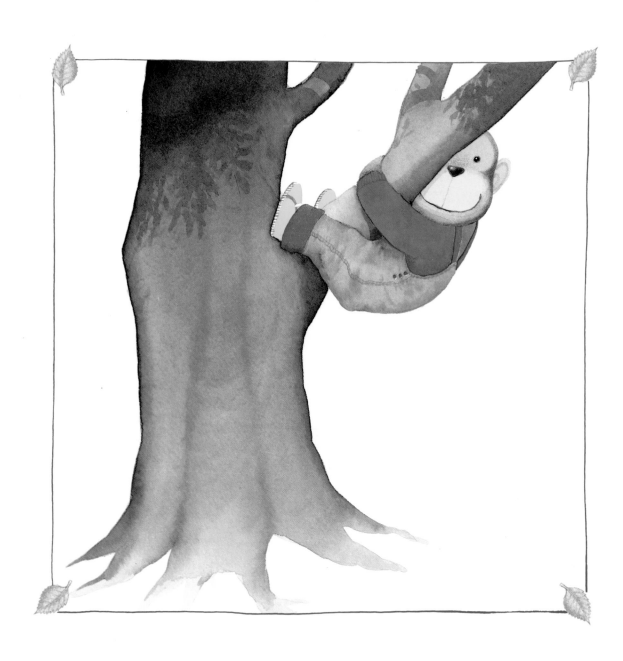

Climbing trees ...

and kicking a ball.

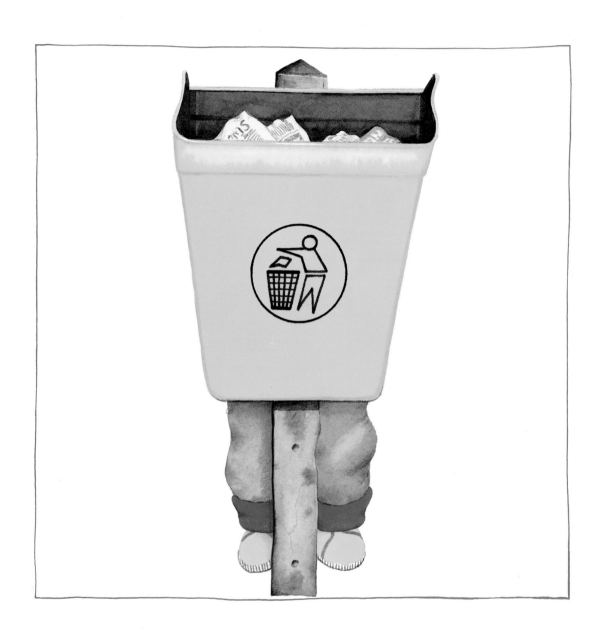

Hiding ...

and acrobatics.

Building sand-castles ...

and paddling in the sea.

Making a cake ...

and watching TV.

Going to birthday parties ...

and being with my friends.

Having a bath ...

hearing a bedtime story ...

and dreaming.

MORE WALKER PAPERBACKS
For You to Enjoy

Also by Anthony Browne

I LIKE BOOKS

A cheeky chimp's introduction to the joy of books.

"Anthony Browne's apparently simple pictures are full of allusive detail…
His wit and invention are unflagging." *Books*

0-7445-5441-1   £4.99

WILLY THE WIMP

The first of the popular tales about the mild chimp,
who always comes out on top.

"A book which made me laugh out loud." *Parents*

0-7445-4363-0   £4.99

PIGGYBOOK

Mr Piggott and his two sons behave like pigs to poor Mrs Piggott – until,
finally, she walks out. Left to fend for themselves, the male Piggotts
undergo some curious changes!

"A superb and unforgettably funny (yet ultimately serious) picture book."
The Good Book Guide

0-7445-3303-1   £4.99

Walker Paperbacks are available from most booksellers, or by post from B.B.C.S., P.O. Box 941, Hull, North Humberside HU1 3YQ
24 hour telephone credit card line 01482 224626

To order, send: Title, author, ISBN number and price for each book ordered, your full name and address,
cheque or postal order payable to BBCS for the total amount and allow the following for postage and packing:
UK and BFPO: £1.00 for the first book, and 50p for each additional book to a maximum of £3.50.
Overseas and Eire: £2.00 for the first book, £1.00 for the second and 50p for each additional book.

Prices and availability are subject to change without notice.